THE ROSE AND • THE PICKLE

To Esme,
You are so Beautiful!
Your Friend,
Adrienne Golday

A TALE OF BEAUTY

Written by ADRIENNE GOLDAY

Illustrated by TAYLOR BARNES

Designed by GARRY TOSTI

WISDOM BOOK PUBLISHERS, INC.
Agoura Hills, California

This book is dedicated to you, the millions of people in this world, who are each unique and magnificent.

To my daughters, Paris and Shayne, and to all people, it is my hope that when you ask, "Who's beautiful?" you will think of *The Rose and the Pickle*, and know the answer.

ISBN 0-930509-00-5
Library of Congress 84-51030
2nd Ed. 1st Printing 1988

1

THE ROSE

I feel wonderful today. The sun is bright and the moist air is cooling, adding a special mist to my body. It is so great to be young and alive and healthy. The breeze is soft and gentle. Oh, what a beautiful morning!

Why, over there are my very good friends the lilies, and across the path are the daisy families. They, too, are feeling good and enjoying this splendid day.

Here comes the little girl who lives in the house at the end of the lane. She is with her mother. Maybe today they will notice how I have grown.

"Oh, what a beautiful rose! Look how pretty it is. It is so soft. Do you see, mommy?"

"Oh, what a beautiful rose! Look how pretty it is. It is so soft. Do you see, mommy?"

"Yes, dear, and it will have a special place on our table tomorrow night. We are having a dinner party. The rose will add just the right touch to the table!"

Tomorrow I will be on their dinner table. I shall be the most beautiful rose anyone has ever seen!

I have been part of this pretty garden, but now I will be enjoyed by the people inside the house. They will admire me. I think tomorrow will be the best day of my life!

CHAPTER TWO

THE
TABLE

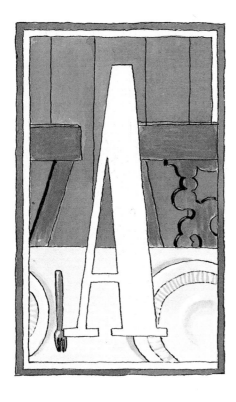

ll of the flowers were very proud of me when I left the garden. Everyone congratulated and complimented me on my magnificence and good fortune. I've been much luckier than many of my friends who were born with tinier and less wholesome bodies. Some did not have the benefit of growing in a

9

On both sides of me, tall candles are glowing, sending a warm light all around me.

sunny garden with rich and fertile soil.

Here I am now in a shiny crystal vase filled with warm water to drink.

Everything else on the table is lovely, also. There is a white linen tablecloth covering the shiny wooden table. On both sides of me, tall candles are glowing, sending a warm light all around me. Fine shiny crystal glasses sparkle beside the china plates. It is the most elegant table.

Oh, no! What is the big, fat, ugly green blob on that plate?

"What on earth is that unsightly thing doing on this lovely table?" Rose exclaimed.

14

CHAPTER THREE

THE PICKLE

hat was that you said?" the pickle asked, awakening from a short nap. "Did I hear you say unsightly? Ugly green blob? I am the most significant delicacy on this table! I come from a fine family, otherwise I could never have been placed in this prestigious company of the finest beef and potatoes."

"I am the most significant delicacy on this table!" said the pickle.

I am a pickle, and the very best of pickles, I'll have you know. When these people taste me tonight, they will feel pleasure they have never before known. And their hunger will be delicately satisfied."

The pickle glared at the rose and continued to defend himself.

"I give energy to the body as well as pleasure. But what would you know of this type of satisfaction? You are here only as mere decoration!"

"If you were not here, then no one would smell your sweet scent. They would only smell my distinctive aroma. And when people smell me their taste buds tingle and they desire me all the more.

"You have the nerve to call me unsightly!

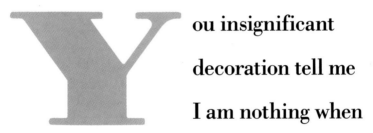You insignificant decoration tell me I am nothing when I satisfy hunger and provide energy, which is life itself, to these fine people.

"What do *you* have to offer?"

A sad silence fell. Two, maybe three moments passed.

Suddenly Rose felt a surge of anger.

It was a feeling she had never known.

She answered. "I am the Great Giver! You merely fill the stomach. And if one received any energy from your odd form, it would be a miracle indeed!

"Even a fine steak that enriches the body could not compare with the enrichment that I give. I enlighten the soul!

"The world needs love. The world needs beauty. I *am* love and beauty. I *am* the food of the soul. And if a soul were hungry, it would *never* desire you, Pickle."

The rose and the pickle felt confused.

Although the rose had quickly defended herself, a feeling of great inadequacy swept through her. She didn't stand quite as tall as she had before. She even felt guilty for putting the pickle in his place, though he did deserve it, she thought.

And the pickle also felt a loss of confidence. He who had been so proud before, lay self-consciously on his plate feeling ugly and unworthy.

Pickle knew that he would never be considered beautiful or something that enriches the soul. He started to feel like an ugly green blob.

21

The lady of the house had been busy all day cleaning so her home would be at its finest for her guests.

CHAPTER FOUR

THE
DINNER

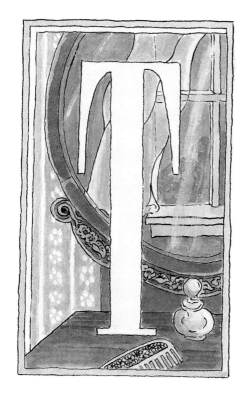

he lady of the
house had been
busy all day
cleaning so her home would be at its finest
for her guests. Then she dressed herself
in a lovely outfit in order to look her
best. The first thing one notices about
the lady of the house are her beautiful,
big, brown eyes.

26

As the lady greeted her first guest, new vibrations seemed to be entering the room.

"Oh," said the guest with the large hat, "Our good friends have this very same style house. Only theirs is furnished with priceless antiques."

The lady of the house replied quickly, "Well, we like ours very much also." But her voice was weak and her big, brown eyes saddened a bit.

The little girl stood by her mother's side. Her hair was chestnut and her eyes were as big as her mother's and browner than a brown crayola.

27

She shyly buried her head in her mother's dress.

The guest with the big hat and superior air continued. "You do look just like your mother, don't you? How old are you?"

But the child did not answer. She shyly buried her head in her mother's dress.

"Oh, you aren't very talkative, are you? You remind me of my niece who is just about your age. Only my niece has the most gorgeous blonde hair and the bluest eyes. Everyone talks about how beautiful she is!"

The little girl looked very sad and did not feel special about herself at all.

On and on the guests talked. Each

passing comment was worse than the last. It seemed that it would never end.

As the rose and the pickle listened in the background, the pickle said to the rose, "Hey, Rose, do you hear how foolish they sound? How do you think that lady made the little girl feel when she talked about her beautiful niece's blonde hair and blue eyes?

"How does one judge beauty, anyway, Rose? I mean that little girl should indeed be considered a beautiful child with her shining hair and bright, big, brown eyes.

31

The little girl looked very sad and did not feel special about herself at all.

"Isn't she lovely, Rose? Who determines what beauty is? Who makes up the standard image of what is beautiful?"

As the people were seated at the table, the pickle continued. "And, Rose, wasn't it unkind of that lady to say what she did to the little girl? Why would she do that?"

"I don't know, Pickle, but I think that she might not have felt very special about herself."

"Yes, Rose, not feeling special about yourself might cause you to hurt others."

"How on earth can beauty be judged? Who can say *this* is beautiful or handsome and *that* is not?" Pickle exclaimed.

The people at the table continued to compare themselves to each other. Ms. White boasted about her decorating work. When Ms. Jones talked about her successful modeling career, Ms. White turned as green as the pickle. And Mr. Smith, who was a businessman, wished he could be a lawyer like Mr. Hill.

The more they talked, the worse they felt. It seemed they each wanted to be something other than what they were.

The people at the table continued to compare themselves to each other.

And the pickle said to the rose:

"Isn't anyone at this table happy? We each have our own special talents. And even though we can't do what the next person does, we can still enjoy his talents as well as our own!

"I mean, if everyone wanted to be a doctor then who would be a plumber or a singer or a rose or a pickle?"

"Gee, Pickle, you're right! I mean, I'm sorry for what I said about you. I've been thinking. You are special! You give immeasurable pleasure to people!"

"And you, Rose, make me feel great when I look at you!"

All of a sudden, Pickle yelled, "Hey, Rose! Someone is picking me up. She is taking a bite!

"Did you hear what she said? 'What a delicious pickle. The best I've ever had.'"

"I heard her, friend, and I'm happy for you. You made her feel really good."

"Look at that gorgeous rose. It is so big and lovely. But I like carnations most of all. Carnations are my favorite flower," one of the guests commented.

"Rose, I'm sorry," Pickle said. "Don't feel bad."

"That's all right, Pickle. I guess everyone can't love me. I mean, I'm a rose, not a carnation *or* a pickle. Isn't that what we just said?"

"Well, my favorite flowers *are* roses," another guest continued. "Why I once saw a rose that was so big and beautiful that everyone talked about it. Everyone turned to notice how magnificent it was!"

And Rose was sad. She felt so inadequate. "I've tried so hard, Pickle. I guess there is always someone who will come along and be more beautiful.

"Well, maybe next time, when I return, I'll be the most beautiful rose ever.

"But...but...next time maybe a bigger and more beautiful rose will come along again and then what?"

Well, the pickle thought and thought.

"I think, my friend, there is no most beautiful or best at anything. You have something special that the bigger rose they mentioned doesn't have. There is no top or best to anything!"

The little girl of the house picked up the vase and took Rose upstairs to her room.

And as the lady took another bite of the pickle, the room filled with his lasting words of great truth...

"I've got it, Rose! I've got the answer! There will never be another pickle like me, ever again! And, you, Rose, your beauty is yours alone and can never again be duplicated."

As Rose thought about what Pickle was saying, the little girl of the house picked up the vase and took Rose upstairs to her room.

And Rose realized what the pickle had said was indeed the answer...

"I am unique! There will never be another rose exactly like me. Beauty cannot be measured."

She stood erect with new found pride. And after all, she thought, no other rose in the world can say she had a pickle for her best friend.

THE END